# Sweet on her Favorite Rancher

### HEATHER SCARLETT

# One

ALEXIA LEWIS DROVE up the winding driveway to the Hudson ranch, her stomach in knots. She gripped the steering wheel with sweating palms as she navigated down the dirt road.

The trees surrounding the drive were more mature than they were twelve years ago, when she first visited. The large wooden sign announcing Hudson ranch was a little more weathered. She supposed she was, as well.

Anticipation settled in the pit of her stomach. She took first one sweaty hand, then the other, off the steering wheel to rub them down her shorts.

What would it be like to see Cameron Hudson again after all these years? She smoothed down her long, dark waves. She couldn't risk a check of her appearance in the rearview mirror since she was driving. While May in Montana wasn't hot, the humidity was rough on her curls. She hoped the extra styling products she'd used today did their job.

She parked the car in her usual spot, along the fence line. Though she supposed it wasn't her usual spot anymore.

Funny, though, how the vehicles in the driveway were unfamiliar, but none were in her spot, as if it was waiting for her.

She remained in the car, gazing ahead at the miles of pasture beyond. Sighing, she placed her hands on the steering wheel, then rested her head on them. She took several deep breaths, willing her racing heart to slow.

Memories flooded of times past. This ranch had been a second home to her, even more welcoming than her own in Seattle. She'd first learned to ride a horse on this ranch, sat down with the family for meals, experienced her first kiss, and fallen in love.

A man stood at the tailgate of an oversized pickup, unloading wood. He hefted a large piece onto his shoulder, and Alexia watched with fascination as his biceps bulged and flexed. He was wearing a tight white tee shirt which emphasized his deep tan. A flush spread from her face down her neck and she shivered. *Who was this man?*

Alexia let her gaze travel from his muscled shoulders down past his trim waist to his thick thighs encased in denim. Maybe there would be a silver lining to helping with the wedding if it meant she might get to know this fine specimen.

A final deep breath and appearance check in the rearview mirror, then she pushed open her car door and got out as gracefully as possible while also pretending she was not ogling the sexy man. Wildwood Falls was a small town and there were few people she didn't know as the owner of the only bakery in town. *How had this man escaped her notice?*

She wished she was the kind of woman to just walk right up to a handsome man and say hello. Opportunity didn't strike too often in her experience. She really should take advantage.

Rather than seize the moment, however, she took the cowardly way out and shifted her gaze away to the barns in the distance. She kicked the toe of her sneaker in the dirt, her hand coming up to absentmindedly twirl a curl.

Heart racing, Alexia debated her next move. Did she go up to the house or should she head for the barn where the wedding would be held? She couldn't awkwardly stand here forever and ignore the stranger. Each moment that ticked past became increasingly uncomfortable.

Before she could decide, the stranger set his load down on the truck bed and made his way over to her. Her skin prickled and her heart threatened to pound out of her chest. *Was it possible to die of anticipation?*

The man approached in long, confident strides and she couldn't help but notice how well he filled out his jeans. The scruff on his jaw gave him a dangerous look. She shivered.

Alexia stood tall, returning her hands to her sides and willing herself to remain in place, even though every instinct said to run. She forced herself to take a deep breath to counter the lightheadedness. Clearly it was possible to die from wanting.

"Alexia?"

She startled at her name, curious how this stranger would know her. She'd have remembered if he came into the bakery.

"Yes, I'm here to work on the wedding favors with Sarah." She silently cursed the squeak in her voice.

"She mentioned that. She's down at the barn. You remember how to get there?" His gaze swept over her, as if he was drinking after a long drought. He swallowed and Alexia watched his adam's apple bob.

"Yes, I do." Alexia studied the man closely. He looked vaguely familiar. Had they met?

His mouth twisted in a wry smile. "I suppose we spent plenty of time down there."

*We?* Then it clicked. This was Cameron. All grown up and hot as a wildfire.

Alexia's heart stopped, then beat wildly at the realization. She'd expected her reunion with Cameron to be awkward since they hadn't seen each other in years and had never really had any closure to their youthful fling. She had not expected it to be awkward because he was the most attractive man she'd ever seen.

And she'd been salivating over him just moments before. This was not going as expected.

"Thanks, Cameron," she replied. "I'll just head down and find Sarah." And her dignity. What was left of it, at least.

* * *

Cameron rubbed the back of his neck as he made a concerted effort to stand upright. Alexia damn near brought him to his knees. She was beautiful at fourteen. She was drop-dead gorgeous now.

He'd known he would see her today. Luke had given him advanced notice of the plan. He'd been prepared. So he thought. There was no way he could have prepared himself for the gut punch that was Alexia all grown up. She'd stood in the dirt, gazing at the pastures, seeming nervous. Then, she'd turned those green eyes on him and he was nearly struck down where he stood. The look of pure attraction rooted him to the spot. It was a wonder he found his voice.

He was tempted to rush to her, pick her up, and spin her in his arms. That had been their standard greeting. It had been seven years, though, so he held back. As he watched Alexia make her way down to the barn, he was reminded of the many times in the past they'd make that trip together. Holding hands, laughing, kissing.

He shook his head, hoping to shake thoughts of Alexia from his memory. He'd been playing their past on an endless loop in his head since she'd left for the last time at nineteen.

And even more since she'd returned. He'd worked hard to avoid her since her return, which was an impressive feat in a small town. The fact that he avoided her for almost a year deserved some kind of prize.

Self-protection drove his avoidance. One which was validated the moment he saw her step out of the car. Long legs in denim cutoffs and a snug tank top. Her dark waves framed her face and tumbled around her shoulders. An image of her hair spread out on the grass as they star-gazed arose, unbidden. He shook it off. It was no secret to him he still had feelings for his first love. He'd like to keep the secret safe from her.

He'd hoped she'd look him up and reconnect when she moved to Wildwood Falls. He's spun fantasies of them confessing their undying love to each other over a reunion dinner. That wasn't to be. She hadn't reached out. So, he avoided her. Obviously, their fling meant more to him than to her.

Cameron entered the barn and dropped his load of wood next to his workspace. Alexia and Sarah were on the other side of the building, near where the wedding supplies were being prepared. His brother, Luke, was marrying the love of his life, Joy, in a few weeks. The women hadn't noticed him come in. Alexia stood next to the arch he was carving as a wedding gift, her fingers tracing the details of the wood.

"This is beautiful," she breathed.

Sarah nodded her agreement. "It is. Cameron does amazing work."

"This is Cameron?!" He was stunned by the wonder evident in Alexia's voice. "It is. I always tell him he should sell his work, but he doesn't. He's too talented to hide his work away in a barn." Cameron never understood when his family make these remarks. To him, his wood carving was a hobby. It got his mind of things. Simple as that.

"He is," Alexia agreed. "I had no idea he did this kind of work. I thought he worked the ranch."

"Oh, he does. The woodworking is in his spare time. Joy says that Luke encourages him to make a living with wood, too. William can always hire extra help for the ranch. And their brother, Dylan, plans to stay here, too."

Cameron bristled at Sarah announcing his business. How did she even know that? He supposed Luke talked to his fiancé and Joy must have shared with her friends. His back muscles tensed at the thought. Did his family sit around talking about his life behind his back? Even though he knew they meant well, the thought rankled.

He turned to sneak out of the barn before he was noticed. As he began to leave, he caught the edge of his hammer and it clattered to the floor. He cursed under his breath. So much for a silent exit.

"Cameron!" Sarah called. "We were just talking about you. Come over and say hi to Alexia. She's here to help."

"I've already said hi," Cameron grunted, admonishing himself for how childish that sounded. He stayed put, neither leaving nor approaching the women. A year of avoiding Alexia, and now he couldn't escape her company.

Given his reaction to her outside, he wasn't sure he was ready to face her again so soon. His mind was a riot of thoughts and he felt emotionally wrung out. He needed some time to think. Alone.

He sighed deeply, resigned that he needed to join them, however briefly. It was not in his nature to be rude, even though it was tempting in this moment. Cameron walked over to Alexia and Sarah, pasting a smile on his face and hoping Alexia wouldn't notice the effect she had on him.

"How's the wedding planning?" He had a pretty good idea given his proximity to the operation, but it was a neutral topic of conversation.

"Great! We finally got all the favors in and are assembling today. It's going to take a while. Griffin is helping Luke with some ranch work, then they'll grill up a feast. You should come by for dinner."

Cameron didn't point out that he lived here and, therefore, was always here for dinner. It was good to know that Alexia would also be there. He might have to change his plans and head to town. Although now that he had an official invite, that might look suspicious. He didn't want Alexia to know he was avoiding her. Hurting her was the last thing he wanted to do.

"I just may do that. I'm not one to turn down good barbecue." Or the craft beer that would likely be available, also, from the new brewery in town. The space had been a brewpub and events center for some time, but recently was purchased by an out-of-town investor who was well known in the San Diego beer scene. No one had met the mystery brewer yet, but the beer was incredible.

"You're staying too, Alexia?" Sarah asked her friend.

"Um, I may have to check something at the bakery...."

"I thought it was closed Mondays?" Sarah focused her sharp gaze on Alexia, who squirmed.

"Oh, well, I guess it can wait. I'll stay." Seems like Alexia was also trying to avoid him. He should be relieved by that knowledge, but instead it made his skin prickle. He shifted from one foot to the other, as he glanced towards the open barn door.

Sarah frowned as she looked between Cameron and Alexia. Finally, she nodded. "Ok, then. I guess we'll get to work. Fair warning, there is plenty of girl talk planned, so you may want to make yourself scarce."

Cameron didn't need to be told twice. He headed out of the barn to the safety of the farthest pasture. Checking fence line was preferable to being close to Alexia. Hopefully hard

labor would clear his head, so he could get his emotions in
check.

# Two

AN AFTERNOON in the sun out in the far pasture had done little to focus Cameron's thoughts. He returned dutifully in time for the barbecue dinner, his stomach doing flip flops. The sun and labor had succeeded in tiring him physically, but done nothing for his thoughts and ricocheting emotions.

The back patio was set up in full party mode, with the beverage cooler stocked and the large grill fired up. With a sigh, Cameron climbed the steps that led to the spacious outdoor patio. He snagged a local lager from the cooler and cracked open the can. He probably should have stopped to shower first, as he was a bit dirty and probably smelled like sweat. Too late for that, as Sarah, Alexia, Luke, and Griffin piled out of the kitchen door, arms laden with food.

The women placed a generous selection of side dishes on the large picnic table, while Luke carried a platter of raw steaks. Likely fresh from the source of Hudson Ranch. Griffin brought up the rear with freshly baked rolls.

Cameron shook his head. His brother's idea of a casual get together was a little extra. His parents had been the head of the ranch until a few months ago, when they took their much-deserved retirement to Coeur d'Alene, Idaho. Now, Luke and Joy lived on the ranch and helped William manage it, including the social calendar, which was always full.

Cameron's chest felt tight at the ease with which his brother welcomed everyone to their family spread. Cameron wished he was half as good as his brother at socializing. Luke had been a champion rodeo star, though, and was very used to being center stage. Cameron was always lost in the shuffle. The middle of four brothers, he spent his life catching up to his older siblings.

Cameron often ended up on the sidelines. Their brother, Dylan, was the youngest and often had the most of their parent's attention. He'd just fallen in love with his best friend after entering a dancing competition a few months ago and was settling into his ranching career.

Their oldest brother, William, was the wild card. He ran the business of the ranch competently, leaving the face of the ranching operations to Luke. William much preferred to avoid socializing and was rarely in attendance at a social function, let alone in the spotlight.

Cameron ambled over to where Luke was now setting steaks on the flames of the grill. "Need help?" He asked, though he knew the answer would be no. Luke took his grilling seriously. He supposed he would, too, if he was solely responsible for raising it from a calf.

"Nah, I'm good, but I could use a beer." Cameron fetched the desired beverage for his brother and set it down on the railing next to the grill. Envy crawled up his spine, not for the first time, when with Luke. He'd never be at ease with himself as his older brother.

"Thanks, man. Can you check on Joy? She wasn't feeling very well earlier and is in the den with lemonade."

Cameron went into the house, secretly glad for an errand

that took him away from the party. He still hadn't figured out how to breathe right around Alexia. She was more stunning than ever and as much as his brain knew she was off limits, the rest of him hadn't gotten the memo.

He found Joy in the den, sipping lemonade and looking rather green.

"You ok?"

The normally perky blond was looking peaked.

"I'm fine. Just feeling tired lately. I'm sure it's wedding stress."

Cameron wasn't at all sure that was the issue, but he would not suggest to his future sister-in-law that perhaps she and Luke were expecting a new family member.

"Anything I can do?" He sincerely hoped not. He was not confident in his ability to handle whatever issue Joy was experiencing.

"I'm fine. I'll be out in a few minutes. This lemonade hits the spot." She settled back on the cushions and closed her eyes.

"Ok, I'll report back to Luke, then." Relieved, Cameron retreated back to the patio to update Luke and rejoin the party. Once there, he was careful to keep a safe distance from Alexia. Just two more weeks and he could go back to pretending they didn't live in the same town.

* * *

Alexia tapped her phone impatiently. She was waiting for Cameron to show up so they could run a wedding errand. *Where was that man?*

The bridal store in town had ordered the veil weeks ago, but because of a last-minute shipping snafu, it was stranded in a New York port with little hope of arriving in time for the wedding. Something about a dock worker strike. So Alexia had volunteered to drive to Spokane, Washington, which was the closest location that Joy could find another of that veil.

Dread settled in her gut like a stone. She'd managed to get through the barbecue with Cameron, but a long car ride in close proximity was a whole different thing. There would be no avoiding.

The sooner he showed, the sooner she'd be done with this ridiculous outing. She had initially planned to drive on her own, but Luke had a last-minute request for his wedding party gifts and asked Cameron to take the ride with Alexia. Now she was stuck in a car with him for at least three hours. Plus, they needed to run several errands in Spokane. Oh, and also pretend that everything between them was perfectly normal. Everyone had a first love, and even though it didn't end the way they would have liked, there was no reason they needed to revisit the past.

Alexia's sole employee bustled out from the kitchen. Mabel was her grandmother's long-time employee, who filled in for Alexia when she needed a hand and was instrumental in the early days after Alexia inherited the bakery from her grandmother. Mabel was 90 if she was a day, yet was as spry as ever.

"Morning, darling. Where are you off to on a Wednesday?" Mabel knew that Alexia rarely took time off.

"I'm off on a wedding errand for Joy," Alexia replied, her eyes scanning the street in front of the bakery.

"That's wonderful," Mabel crooned, as she moved behind the counter and donned the signature bakery apron. "Go on, now, I've got things under control here."

Alexia knew that Mabel did. "I'm just waiting on Cameron," she replied, as she cast another glance through the bakery's picture window.

"Cameron, oh my!" Mabel exclaimed. "He's a handsome one. I hadn't realized this was a date."

"No date. Just two members of the wedding party running errands."

"Uh, huh. Well, you look awfully dressed up for errands."

Alexia bristled. She was wearing a bit more makeup than usual and a cute summer sundress. But she was going to the big city, after all. She'd dress the same whether or not she was going with Cameron. *Wouldn't she?*

"It's just Cameron. We're old friends."

Mabel smiled a knowing smile. "Yes, dear, old friends are the best friends and you two go way back. ..."

"That we do." Alexia wondered what would be different if she hadn't taken the college internship and instead returned for another summer in Wildwood Falls. Would Cameron have proposed? Would she have had the courage to defy her parents and say yes?

She'd never know because she did take the internship. Then, accepted a full time job after graduation. Met Chad and dated him through her last two years of college. Assumed her life was figured out as she had a good job lined up and a future husband. When he dumped her on their graduation day, she was stunned. Her carefully curated life seemed to be falling apart. Then, her grandmother died and Alexia inherited the bakery and her grandmother's small house. Despite her parent's objections, she leapt at the chance to start over in Wildwood Falls.

The roar of a truck engine pulled Alexia from her thoughts. Mabel was right that she did have a history with Cameron. One she'd wished to revisit at one time in her life. Not now, though. Too much time had passed for her to have any hope they had a chance. She feared she'd hurt him too much.

"Thanks for watching the bakery, Mabel. I'll see you later."

Mabel smiled. "Don't worry about me. I'll lock up at six as

always and have everything set for you in the morning. Enjoy your trip." She winked at Alexia, then turned back to the bakery case and fussed over placing the eclairs.

Alexia smiled softly. Her grandmother had been particular about the eclairs, as well. It touched her to see Mabel take the same care.

The door chimed and when she looked up, Cameron's large frame filled the doorway. He seemed even larger when compared to the modest doorway. Her breath caught.

He wore dark jeans and a forest green henley that brought out his eyes. Alexia forgot to breathe when he reached up to rest his hand on the top of the frame, emphasizing his long, lean physique.

"Are you ready?" he asked, almost shyly. His eyes darted around the bakery, taking stock of the familiar surroundings. Alexia had changed nothing since taking over from her grandmother, so she could imagine Cameron was thinking of when they were in high school and spent so much time here. Did he have the same positive memories as she did? Hours of eating bakery snacks and holding hands at the table in the window. How far they'd come from that enamored young couple.

Love had proven to be harder to sustain than they expected. *Not exactly,* her heart reminded her. She knew she'd loved Cameron, but no one expected adolescent love to last. And she'd needed to focus on her college education and her future. At least that's what her parents had convinced her when they discouraged her from spending so much time with her grandmother summers off from college. Much better to focus on the future, not the past, they'd said.

And Alexia had believed them. Until her grandmother become ill and died and she realized her heart had always and forever been in Wildwood Falls. Her future belonged there.

She'd once hoped that future would be spent with

Cameron, but even though it hadn't turned out that way, Wildwood Falls would always be home.

# Three

SHE AND CAMERON had been driving about an hour on interstate 90, going west. They had about thirty minutes before Spokane, and it couldn't come fast enough. They'd been quiet for most of the drive once they'd run through the pleasantries about weather and traffic.

Alexia glanced at Cameron, his firm jaw silhouetted in the sunlight. What she would have given at sixteen to escape the city with him for a few hours. Back then, they'd stolen time in the bed of his pickup looking at stars.

She glanced behind her at the bed of his extended-cab truck. Newer and in much better condition than the one he drove when they were teenagers. Shiny black with flecks of sparkle and silver rims that reflected the sunlight. It wasn't the truck he drove for daily ranch work, she knew, because those vehicles got beat up. This was his driving to town truck. *Had he washed it just for this trip?* She thought he might have, as it was so shiny and clean.

Her stomach tumbled at the thought he'd done something specific for her. It was just a trip to Spokane; she reminded herself. Not a date. Purely coincidence that he'd washed his truck. Just like it was coincidental she'd dressed up for the occasion.

When the sign for the wedding boutique came into view, Alexia breathed a sigh of relief. Just a little longer and they'd be back on the road home. Then she could escape from the constant stream of memories that pulled her in like quicksand.

The nights spent watching stars. Dreaming of the future. A future that Alexia thought was a distant hope, but Cameron clearly expected to be an immediate reality. Alexia remembered finding the engagement ring in his drawer when he asked her to retrieve a tee shirt after they'd been caught in an unexpected summer storm. Her heart had stopped, then thundered out of control. They were only nineteen. Too young for those kind of permanent promises.

When the internship offer came along the next summer, that ring haunted her. She was reminded of the poem about two roads diverging. Return to Wildwood Falls and marry Cameron or take the coveted internship and remain in Seattle. She chose Seattle and would forever be haunted by the what ifs. What if she'd returned. What if he proposed? And she said yes? They might be driving together, just like this, except with a family in the seats behind them.

Alexia got chills at the thought. Her and Cameron married, with a family.

As the bridal boutique was located downtown, it took Cameron a few minutes to locate parking. His large truck was difficult to park in a congested downtown. Finally, he found a spot the truck could fit. Thankfully, there was an app and there was no need for coins.

They walked the distance to the shop in silence. Alexia glanced around, noting various trendy shops and restaurants. The bridal store was between a gourmet bakery and a fancy espresso bar. Alexia lingered at the large display window of the bakery, cataloguing ideas.

Cameron noticed her close observation of the display. "You could totally do that if you wanted," he offered as he stopped to stand by her in front of the window.

"I was thinking of it, but not sure if there would be interest from customers."

"Are you kidding? The citizens of Wildwood Falls would clamor for specialty cakes like these."

Alexia cocked her head as she studied the elaborate cakes. "I suppose so. I'd need to hire additional help if I wanted to expand the operation," she acknowledged. "I'm not sure how I feel about that."

Cameron turned a measured look on her. "It's a great idea. You need help as it is. Why not invest in your business? Your grandmother would want to see you happy."

At the mention of her grandmother, Alexia sighed. Her grandmother had been the force behind the bakery for as long as Alexia could remember. She'd done things old school and had managed with minimal help all these years. Would Alexia be able to live up to her grandmother's memory?

"What about you, Cameron? What about your dreams?"

He turned to face her. "What dreams do you mean?"

"Your wood carvings are beautiful. When you you going to pursue your art?"

"It's a hobby, Alexia. Not a career."

"It could be." She wasn't sure why she was pushing him, except it was easier than dealing with her own resistance to change.

"You sound like my family." An accusation. Not untrue. She agreed with them he should pursue his creative endeavor.

Alexia shrugged. "I think you should consider it. You could make a living doing something you enjoy."

Cameron shook his head. "I'm happy the way things are now. No need to change."

Ah, that word again. Change. It's what kept her frozen for so long, until circumstances forced her to re-imagine her future. If only Cameron could do the same.

Alexia knew in her heart her grandmother would be happy for her. Like Cameron said, she'd be happy that Alexia was growing the business and making a comfortable living. Alexia had trouble shaking the guilt that always crawled up her spine when she contemplated change. The familiar was comfortable. She hated the possibility that she'd let down someone she cared about.

Which was why she'd walked away from Wildwood Falls all those years ago. Following her parents' dreams for her was comfortable, as much as she despised their vision of her life. It was easier to go along than to stand up to them. Once she realized how serious Cameron was about their future, she'd felt unprepared to make that kind of commitment. So, she walked backwards into comfort instead of forward into hope.

Even if it meant leaving Cameron, the love of her life, behind.

She'd never explained that to him back then. She didn't have the words. Over the years, she'd contemplated trying, because she hated that she'd left him hanging. Wondering. Though she supposed he'd moved on, just as she had. Not that he was seeing anyone. Nor was she.

She shook her head to shake those dangerous thoughts free. Cameron was still the same as always. Set in his plans for the future, no matter how unrealistic. If he couldn't imagine a different future for himself, how could she expect him to be open minded about a shared future?

"We should get the veil before your parking expires. We still need to pick up the groomsmen gifts before we leave."

Cameron hesitated before agreeing. "You're right. Let's

go." He opened the door to the bridal shop and held it for Alexia. She gave the bakery display one more longing look before she proceeded Cameron into the store.

* * *

Cameron reluctantly followed Alexia into the bridal salon, momentarily losing his nerve and almost turning around and waiting on the sidewalk. Alexia looked no more confident than him, as she took in the tulle-filled space that was overwhelmingly, blindingly white. Wedding dresses on racks along the walls and several displays of headpieces.

A woman approached, a wide smile on her face. "Can I help you find something?"

Alexia found her voice before Cameron. "Yes, we're picking up a veil."

"Ah yes, that makes sense," the woman crooned. "It would be very unusual for a groom to escort the bride to choose her wedding gown. Though times are changing, I suppose."

"No wedding gown for me. I'm picking up a veil for my friend."

The woman's mouth twisted in confusion. "For your friend? What about you? Have you chosen your gown yet? If not, we have many to select from."

"Oh no, I'm not getting married. I'm the maid of honor."

The woman's eyes darted between Alexia and Cameron. "Oh, I'm so sorry. I just assumed you two were a couple."

Cameron felt his face flush with embarrassment. He cleared his throat to dislodge the panic that had settled there. "No, not at all. Just the wedding party helping our friends."

Alexia nodded vigorously. "Just doing our wedding party duty," she agreed. He didn't want the woman to assume they were a couple, but the way Alexia corrected her so quickly gave the impression the suggestion appalled her. That shouldn't matter to him, but it did.

Her past rejection still stung as fresh as if it were yesterday. *How would it have felt if you were on your knees with a ring?*

Cameron could only imagine the pain if Alexia had rejected a proposal. He hadn't even had the chance to ask.

Alexia gave Joy's order information, and soon the woman returned with a large box.

"This is the veil. But I want to be sure it's the correct length when the bride is in her dress and heels." She pinned Alexia with a sharp look. "Since the bride isn't available to try it on, you'll have to step in."

"Wha... what?!" Alexia replied. "I can't try on another bride's dress."

"Well, dear, it's not her exact dress. It's a similar style. Just to be sure. I may need to make alterations so it's as perfect as possible for her special day."

Alexia nodded in resignation. "Ok, show me to the dressing room." She cast a glance at Cameron. "You can pick up the groomsmen gifts, if you like. Save us time."

Cameron didn't need to be asked twice. He turned and nearly ran out of the store. The idea of seeing Alexia in a wedding dress made him itchy.

Too many memories of what could have been, he supposed. When he'd been nineteen, he'd spent plenty of time picturing Alexia in a wedding dress. On their wedding day. A daydream that was not meant to be.

Cameron took his time picking out groomsmen gifts, as Luke had instructed. Luke had already ordered engraved whiskey tumblers, but left the accessories to Cameron. A set of whisky stones to cool the drink without diluting and a bag of gourmet mixed nuts rounded out each groomsman's gift bag.

*What if Cameron were planning his own wedding?* And

Alexia was trying on her own gown and veil? No sense focusing on what wasn't going to be. He'd learned years ago that it's better to live in the present than an imaginary future.

His errand was over quicker than he expected, since his destination was only a few doors down the street. He pulled open the bridal salon door, eyes on the ground. Surely Alexia was in the back somewhere for the fitting so it would be safe to enter and sit on one of the chaise lounges towards the center of the store.

He dared a glance around and confirmed with relief that the shop was empty. He relaxed onto the chaise, setting the bag of groomsman gifts on the floor beside him, and closed his eyes a moment to enjoy the peace.

"What do you think?" The voice startled Cameron from his reverie. His eyes flew open to see Alexia in front of him, in full bridal regalia. She wore a white dress with a full skirt that highlighted her trim waist. Her ample curves spilled out over the neckline and offered a tantalizing glimpse.

Cameron's heart stopped fully, then started pounding. He gulped air, desperate to fill his lungs as if he was the one wearing the restricting garment.

Both women's eyes were trained on him, awaiting his verdict. Alexia looked guarded, a hot flush on her cheeks. The proprietor was smiling broadly, anticipating his reaction.

"You look..." Cameron paused, unsure of the right word. Pretty seemed too simple. Beautiful, not enough to capture how she looked. "You look stunning." It was true. He'd never seen Alexia in anything more than jeans and practical shirts, often flannel. Seeing her like this, dressed up, looking so... bridal, brought back a flood of memories. Of dreams unrealized. Of the ring still tucked away in his dresser drawer. Waiting. For what, he didn't know. It wasn't destined to be Alexia's, as he once thought, but he couldn't bring himself to sell it.

He pictured the ring and imagined what it might look like on her finger while she wore that dress. Walking down the aisle to him.

"See, I told you. You're stunning in white. You've rendered your man speechless," the woman cooed at Alexia.

"He's not my man," Alexia corrected as Cameron said, "I'm not hers." Although in his heart, he knew he was lying.

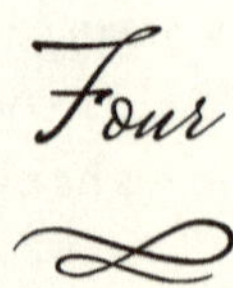

Four

ALEXIA STARED at the window of Cameron's truck, grateful for every mile that brought them closer to Wildwood Falls. The afternoon had been a trial. Too many memories brought up between her and Cameron. Being in a wedding salon, while in a wedding dress, cut far too close to the future she'd walked away from. She didn't regret not marrying Cameron at twenty. She did regret losing a good friend.

Present day Alexia wouldn't mind a second chance at forever with Cameron, but she suspected it was too late to mend the past hurts.

Alexia's stomach growled, and Cameron grinned at her.

"Hungry, Lexie?" Her heart fluttered at his old nickname for her.

"Yeah, I guess I am."

"We should stop for dinner." He shot her a playful look. "I have an idea."

Alexia narrowed her eyes. "Will I like this plan?"

Cameron looked away from the road to shoot her another rogue-ish grin. "You will."

"How can you be so sure?" she asked.

"Because I know you. And I know what you like." Cameron winked, then turned his attention back to the road.

Alexia sat back against the leather seats and resigned herself to a surprise. She knew Cameron enough to know that he wouldn't give her more information. This was so much like the times in high school, during those hot summers, when she and Cameron would drive aimlessly, talking about everything, then stop for fast food at the local burger drive thru. Then, they'd drive out one of the service roads on his family's ranch and park. Cameron would lower the tailgate of the truck, pile the bed with blankets he stowed behind the seats, and they'd eat their dinner under the stars.

They did a lot more than eat dinner on those nights. She and Cameron would lie in the truck's bed, talking, laughing, and kissing. Sighing, Alexia absentmindedly touched her fingers to her lips. Can't go back. The past is the past and those days are long gone.

Cameron had wanted more than she was willing to offer back then. Now? She was ready to settle down but he seemed to have moved on to a different goal. He was focusing on his woodworking business and barely had time for that side hustle, let alone a relationship.

Even if he did, would he end up like her parents? Pushing her faster than she wanted to go and in the wrong direction?

Cameron slowed the truck and took a right turn. Glancing up, Alexia realized they were turning down the street of their favorite burger joint. Were they getting dinner there? Her mouth watered at the prospect.

She hadn't expected Cameron to be so sentimental. Given that he seemed to talk to her as little as humanly possible, she'd assumed that he wanted to keep a firm boundary around their past. Not to bring past sentiment straight into their present reality.

Sure enough, he turned into the parking lot of the Burger

on the Range, a local Wildwood Falls institution. The large bison on the sign was a local landmark. He pulled into the drive thru line, turning to check in with her.

"This ok?" Was it her imagination, or did he look hesitant?

"Are you kidding? This is amazing! I didn't think you remembered."

Cameron shook his head. "How could I not remember? Those were some of the best times of my life."

Alexia smiled. "Mine too."

A tinny voice interrupted their moment. "... your order??"

Cameron rattled off their usuals. A double cheeseburger for him, a bacon burger for her, and an order of large fries to share. Two chocolate milkshakes completed their order. He looked at her for confirmation and Alexia nodded. When riding shotgun with your high school summer love, you went all in with the memories.

They picked up their food from the window and Cameron paid before she had a chance to protest. Butterflies flitted in her stomach at the swift turn of events.

"Thank you," she said as she took the bag Cameron handed her. He placed the drinks in the cup holders between them and she took the straws from the bag and put them in the shakes, just as she always had.

Cameron pulled out of the lot and steered the truck towards the familiar road leading to his ranch. She had left her car there, so it made sense they would head that way after getting food. Maybe they could eat together before she got in her car to head home. She considered asking him, but didn't want to make things awkward between them.

It was ridiculous that the store owner had assumed they were the bride and groom. Wouldn't that be ridiculous? The two of them getting married. It didn't seem so ridiculous ten years ago. Alexia shook her head to clear her thoughts. No sense going back. Cameron wasn't going that way and he'd made that very clear.

The truck entered the driveway of Hudson Ranch and Cameron steered the truck under the large wooden sign with the family's brand. Instead of continuing up the main driveway as she'd expected, he turned off to the left onto the dirt service road that led to the field on the highest point on the ranch.

He didn't say a word as they drove the five minutes over a bumpy dirt road. Alexia held her breath. They were heading for their spot. The field where they parked for hours and shared hopes and dreams. And passionate kisses.

Cameron cleared the ridge and pulled the truck to a stop and turned off the engine. He got out of the truck and Alexia followed, bringing the food and shakes as she had a hundred times before. Cameron reached behind the seat to pull blankets out and spread them in the truck's bed. He popped the tailgate and gestured to Alexia to get in first. She put the food down on the tailgate and then hopped up into the bed of the truck. She settled into the blankets and pulled the food closer as Cameron joined her. They leaned against the cab of the truck and stretched their legs out. Alexia handed Cameron his shake and burger, then took her own. The bag of fries sat between them.

Dusk was just falling and Alexia looked over the valley below, bathed in golden light. She took a bite of her burger and savored the memories. Even though she lived in Wildwood Falls, she couldn't remember the last time she'd taken the drive just outside of town to Burger on the Range. It was really because it wasn't the same without Cameron. All those memories of summers past were best savored with her first love.

They ate in silence, the only sounds the slurp of the straw or the crinkle of the burger wrapper.

Alexia broke the silence. "This is nice."

Cameron nodded. "It is. I hope you don't mind. I haven't been up here in years to watch the sunset and I thought it would be a pleasant way to end the day."

"It is. I forget how beautiful this valley is. And how amazing these burgers are."

Her tongue darted out to catch a stray bit of barbecue sauce and she watched Cameron's eyes follow the movement. Tension snapped between them, electric with promise.

They stared at each other for a long moment, the possibility hanging in the air. Was Cameron going to kiss her?

He leaned forward slightly. *Was he going to kiss her?* Then, he suddenly grabbed fries from the bag between them and stuffed them into his mouth. Silly Alexia, she chided herself. He was just reaching for fries. Her heart sank, and she hadn't even realized it had been rooting for a kiss.

* * *

Cameron couldn't believe he almost kissed Alexia. What was he thinking? Sure, the attraction between them was undeniable, but so was the fact she walked away from their relationship without so much as a backward glance. Coming up here had been a mistake and kissing her would absolutely be a major mistake. The best thing would be to get as far away from her as possible and stay there until all this wedding business was over. That had to be why his head was all over the place today.

Spending hours in the car with Alexia, then going into the bridal store and been mistaken for the bride and groom had been too much for him. While he'd laughed it off, it hit too close to home. He thought of the engagement ring he still kept in his sock drawer. He and Alexia could have been a bride and groom. They could have been a family. If only she'd come back for the summer instead of bailing on him with no explanation.

That had to be why he suddenly had the urge to bring her back here. To revisit the old days. To what could be. But never would be. Though he wished for answers, Cameron was too proud to ask.

Alexia clearly didn't have the same feelings as he did back then, or she'd never have left. Or she would have kept in touch. She could have looked him up when she returned to Wildwood Falls. Or any number of things that didn't involve ghosting him after they declared their love for each other.

"Is everything ok?" Alexia's voice was heavy with concern. And unasked questions.

"Yeah, I was just thinking about the past for a moment." Why did he admit that? No sense ruining this truce between them with old memories.

Alexia put down her shake and turned to face him. "We had a good time those summers," she began. "I..."

Cameron couldn't bear to hear what she said next. He'd been living with her silent rejection all these years and didn't need to hear it said out loud. "We had fun and now that I'm older I understand we were just kids... too young to make the promises we did."

"*That* we were," Alexia acknowledged. "That doesn't mean it wasn't special to me." She reached out and took Cameron's hand. "You meant a lot to me."

"Yet you walked away." The words tumbled out of his mouth without his permission. He hated the vulnerability in his voice. Hated that she would hear it and pity him.

"It wasn't as simple as that," she replied, as she leaned closer. "Look at me."

Cameron raised his eyes to meet hers, surprised to see unshed tears.

"Cameron, I wanted to come back so badly, but my parents wanted other things for me. I was at their mercy. They funded my education, my housing, everything. If I'd disobeyed them, they would have cut me off. Then what?"

*Then you could have stayed with me.*

Thankfully, his brain kept that thought to itself.

"You could have come back for the summer at least."

Alexia shook her head. "No, I couldn't. I had a prestigious internship lined up and needed to stay in Seattle."

"You could have told me."

"You're right, I should have. I wrote letters, then ripped them up. I didn't know how to tell you I couldn't be the person you wanted me to be... and I was avoiding the pain."

"If you cared as much as you said you did, you would have told me." Cameron fought back his own tears that threatened to spill.

"I was young and selfish. I'm sorry I hurt you. I was hurting, too."

"You didn't reach out when you moved back." A stray tear slipped down his cheek, and Alexia reached up to wipe it away with her finger.

"I didn't. I figured you hated me, and it was better that we just moved on."

"I could never hate you."

"You didn't come to see me. You're the only person in Wildwood Falls who doesn't frequent the bakery. I mean, you avoid the only donuts in town because you don't want to see me."

Cameron huffed a small laugh. "I thought you didn't want to see me. You walked away, not me."

"True, but I didn't mean to walk away forever." Alexia paused to take a deep breath. "I hoped when I came back to town we could rekindle our friendship."

"We were never friends." Alexia blanched at Cameron's harsh words. "You know we were way more than friends," Cameron said before he leaned forward and claimed her lips in a searing kiss.

# Five

CAMERON'S LIPS claimed hers with no hesitancy. His arms pulled her close, a hand tangling in her hair. Alexia's heart hammered in her chest. This was really happening.

She cupped his face with her free hand, luxuriating in the feel of his stubble under her fingers. Soft, but just a little scratchy. A new texture from the boy she'd known, who was always clean-shaven.

His lips were soft and insistent as they explored hers. His tongue licked the seal of her lips, gaining entry into her mouth. All Alexia could feel was heat and long-restrained passion in the kiss.

Cameron kissed her as if it were essential to breathing. As if he would expire if not for her lips on his. Alexia understood the sentiment as she couldn't imagine how she survived without his lips pressed to hers.

They were lost in the kiss for long moments, until Cameron finally pulled away, gently.

"I've been thinking about that all day," he breathed against her hair.

"Me, too," Alexia admitted.

Cameron pulled her against his side. "This is where you belong."

"Yes," Alexia agreed. She didn't know how it could possibly work out, but in this moment, this man felt like home. There was no denying how she felt.

Her chest pinched at the thought. Home had never been a comforting thought for her. It came with obligations and strings attached.

What Cameron was offering her now was a different kind of home than she was used to. The sheer comfort of it was terrifying.

She sat next to Cameron, gazing at the dark sky and bright stars above, prolonging this magical moment. Alexia knew her reality would snap back once they left the cozy confines of the truck bed.

She had no idea where they went from here. A few intense kisses didn't establish them as a couple. As much as she wanted that, she didn't want to presume what Cameron wanted.

She'd hurt him. She'd left him without explanation, so she wanted to take his lead this time and give him what he needed.

"It seems we both let ourselves get in the way of our happiness," he said as he pulled her closer to his side.

"We did," Alexia agreed.

"I'd like to get to know you better, Alexia. As we are now."

"I'd like that too."

"I know you're already coming to the wedding, but would you consider coming as my date?"

Alexia's stomach flipped. "Your date?"

"I mean, only if you want to," Cameron hedged.

"I very much want to be your date," Alexia breathed.

Cameron's grin lit up his face. "Good. It will be worth getting all dressed up for you."

"Wait a minute," Alexia said. "What about your family? If

I'm your date, they'll have questions. I mean, they know we used to date... how will they feel about us getting back together?"

"Are we back together?" he asked hesitantly.

Alexia met his steady gaze. "I'd like to be..."

Cameron smiled broadly.

"I'm proud to have you as my date," he said. "And I hope the wedding is the first of many dates to come."

Alexia let out a breath she hadn't realized she'd been holding. "Me, too." Her heart threatened to burst with joy. She'd barely dared to hope Cameron would forgive her. That he was willing to give them a second chance was unbelievable. Alexia was counting the days until the wedding.

* * *

The day of the wedding promised to be a top-ten day of the year. The weather was predicted to be low eighties, with a light breeze and plenty of sunshine. Alexia woke with excitement thrumming through her veins. She barely needed her usual morning coffee before she was ready to head out the door. She was meeting Joy and the other bridesmaids at Hudson Ranch for brunch and to get ready. Her dress was already there, so she just needed to bring herself.

When she arrived at the ranch, the wedding preparations were in full swing. There was no sign of Cameron as she parked in front of the house. She walked up the hill to the ceremony site before joining her friends in the house. As she reached the crest of the hill, the expanse of Wildwood Falls greeted her below. Framing the perfect view was the wooden archway Cameron had carved. The arch was covered in flowers and in the center, framed by his masterpiece, was Cameron. He stood with his back to Alexia, gazing down at the town.

He hadn't heard her come up behind him, so she took advantage of the moment to watch him undetected. Cameron stood tall and proud, his hands on his hips. He was nearly as tall as the structure.

Alexia deliberately made her footsteps known so as not to startle him. "Hello," she called as she approached.

Cameron turned, his smile broadening when he recognized her. "Alexia! I wasn't expecting to see you until I walked you down the aisle."

His choice of words was casual, but they struck a deep chord. It was true he'd be walking her down the aisle at Joy and Luke's wedding today, but somehow all Alexia could think about was walking down the aisle at their own wedding. Which was ridiculous because they'd never talked seriously about marriage and never been engaged.

"I came up to look at your work." She ran her hand along the intricate wood carvings. "It's really beautiful. How come you never went into business for yourself?"

Cameron hesitated as he turned to look back over the valley below. "I have a responsibility to my family's ranch. My woodworking is just a hobby."

"It doesn't have to be a hobby. It could be a career. You're really talented, Cameron. Your work would sell in those fancy boutiques we saw in Spokane."

"I don't want to let my brothers down. William worked so hard to keep this place going after our parents retired. Luke and Dylan both give so much. I'd feel guilty if I didn't pull my weight."

"Have you ever talked to your brothers about it? They may not need you full-time. They could always hire help to fill in the gaps."

"I love this ranch," Cameron said. His way of closing out the conversation. Alexia knew he wouldn't want to talk further on the topic. It was his brother's wedding day, so she let it go. She was sad that he couldn't see his talent and wasn't willing to consider something different from his present circumstances.

She took a tremendous risk moving to Montana permanently to take over the bakery. There were stressful moments, for sure, but she never doubted her decision. She loved her bakery and the opportunity to carry on her grandmother's tradition. There was an art to baking just as to woodworking. She'd tried to deny her creative side for so long, until her grandmother's death. Alexia was grateful she had the opportunity to do something she loved while also making a living. It was a long way from the soul-numbing corporate jobs her parents forced her to take.

Alexia's phone buzzed with a text from Sarah. "I better get to the house and meet the girls. They're about to send out a search party for me," Alexia teased. She knew she needed to go but wasn't ready. She wished she and Cameron could stay up here longer, just the two of them.

"Ok, then. See you at the wedding." Cameron grinned, and Alexia's heart melted. She turned away towards the path down the hill. Cameron gently tugged her arm, which propelled her back towards him. He kissed her long and hard before letting her go. "Just giving you something to remember me by until you see me again," he said with a wink.

She would definitely remember that kiss. In fact, she thought about it all the way down the hill, across the yard, and into the house. She thought about it while her hair and makeup were being done and when they dressed in their bridesmaid dresses. And when they walked Joy to the clearing for the ceremony. She thought about it until she was at the head of the aisle and Cameron appeared beside her, transformed in fitted gray pants and vest, and lavender button down, and matching tie. Something about seeing him out of character, dressed up in a suit with those lavender sleeves rolled up to display the taut muscles of his forearm, set Alexia off balance.

"Ready?" he asked as he offered his arm to her.

Alexia smiled. "Ready as I'll ever be."

# Six

CAMERON HAD an out-of-body experience walking Alexia down the aisle. At least that's how he felt, given the time passed in a breath and he parted with her too soon as they approached the officiant. She looked beautiful this evening in her lavender strapless gown. He was so used to seeing her in casual clothes and no makeup that he lost his breath when she appeared beside him to walk down the aisle. Her long hair had been curled and styled; her makeup was flawless, making her green eyes pop. Cameron resisted the urge to kiss her, right then and there.

The ceremony passed in a blur of happy tears and joyful moments. Before he realized it, he was offering his arm to Alexia a second time as they made their way back up the aisle to the receiving line, where he hugged her against him to greet the guests.

To his right stood his brother, William, looking uncomfortable in the suit and tie. Cameron watched as he shifted from foot to foot, scrubbing his hand over his full beard.

He didn't think he'd ever seen William in anything other than work jeans and a flannel shirt. Maybe a tee shirt on hot days. And his ever-present cowboy hat. Tonight, his head was bare, and Cameron noted he was due for a haircut. He made a mental note to nudge William to town one day next week. If Cameron didn't remind William to take care of himself, he often didn't. Which was another reason he was hesitant to leave the ranch. Who would take care of William if he didn't?

Cameron held onto Alexia as guests filed down the aisle. His brothers shot him a questioning look but said nothing. Before the night was over, they would. Of that, Cameron had no doubt. He didn't care. He had another chance with Alexia, and he was going to take it. And he damn well didn't care what anyone else thought.

A few high school friends passed through the receiving line. Cameron offered handshakes and small talk before passing them down towards the groom. Luke was glowing with happiness and Joy looked radiant beside him. Thankfully, she was having a good day. Even though she hadn't admitted to being pregnant, he suspected they would have a new addition to the family before the year was out.

"Are you going to introduce us to your girlfriend?" a voice boomed in Cameron's ear, forcing his attention back to the present moment. A couple who were good friends with his parents waited eagerly for his response. Oh. They assumed Alexia was his girlfriend. He didn't mind, but it was very early for him to give their relationship that label.

"This is Alexia," Cameron said. Alexia turned and smiled at the couple.

"It's good to meet you," she replied. She shifted her position and Cameron could tell she was uncomfortable with the attention.

The older man, Mr. Branson, was undeterred. "Are you two lovebirds the next to be married?" he asked with a grin.

Oh no. How to get out of this one? Before Cameron

could respond, his mother overheard the comment and interjected. "Who's getting married now? One of your children?"

Mr. Branson laughed. "Oh no, they're all married already. I was asking Cameron if he and his girlfriend would be the next to be married."

His mother turned a shocked look on him. "Cameron? Something you need to tell us?" He watched his mother's eyes dart to Alexia, scanning her midsection before returning to him.

"No, Mom. You remember Alexia? From when we were younger? She used to summer here."

His mother turned once again to Alexia, peering around Dylan and William to do so. "Hello, Alexia. It's lovely to see you again. Did I hear something about a wedding?"

Alexia flushed, and Cameron scrambled to do damage control. The Bransons were standing in front of him still, and the entire receiving line had paused to hear the conversation.

"Mom, no wedding. We'll talk later. Let's allow these guests to get to the reception."

His mom gave him and Alexia one more lingering look before turning back to the receiving line. William cast him a puzzled look, but thankfully Joy and Luke were blissfully oblivious to the brief drama.

"Sorry about that," he whispered to Alexia under his breath. She gave a brief nod of acknowledgement and they continued to greet guests until the last one moved on to the cocktail hour in the barn.

Once the guests left, the family relaxed and dispersed from their formal line. It did not surprise Cameron when his mother made a beeline for him and Alexia.

"So, what was I hearing about a wedding?" she asked.

Cameron sighed. "Mom, Mr. Branson just asked a question. There's no marriage happening."

He saw Alexia flinch.

"Mom, we just agreed to date again. No pressure, ok?"

At those words, his entire family turned to him.

"You and Alexia are dating?!" Joy squealed. She pulled away from Luke to wrap her friend in a hug. "Why didn't you tell me?"

Alexia returned the hug. "It's your big day. I didn't want to take away from that. This is a very new... development."

Cameron could tell Alexia was uncomfortable with all attention focused on them. "She's right, Joy. It's your special day. We don't want to detract from that."

Joy waved her hand as if to wave away the objections. "That's silly. We're happy for you."

Cameron met each of his brother's eyes. How would they react to this news? They watched him wait hopefully for Alexia to return and were witnesses to the heartbreak when she didn't.

William was the first to step forward to shake his hand. "Good for you, brother. I'm glad you're happy." Luke and Dylan followed suit. His parents nodded their approval.

Cameron let a sigh of relief escape. He hadn't realized he worried about their response until now. He let out a breath he didn't realize he was holding when they accepted this news. *How would they react if you told them you wanted to pursue your own business?* His mind interjected that question. One thing at a time.

"I am happy." He took Alexia's hand and smiled at her. She returned the smile, and he felt the tight band around his heart loosen, just a little.

Alexia gripped his hand, and it gratified him that everything seemed to work out alright.

"Time to get to the reception," Luke said, which started the family in motion down the hill towards the barn.

Cameron slowed his walk to allow him and Alexia some

privacy after the family jostled their way down the hill to the celebration.

"How are you feeling?" he asked, as he gave her fingers a quick squeeze.

"Good, I'm glad your family took the news well. And that Joy and Luke didn't mind us announcing it on their big day."

"They're happy for me. What about your family? When are you planning to tell them?"

"I'm not sure," Alexia hedged. "I'm supposed to visit them in a few weeks."

"That's perfect. Do you want company?"

Alexia paused, and Cameron regretted the impulsive offer. Her expression said she clearly did not want company.

"It's probably better that I do this myself," she replied, a tactful dodge. Cameron let it go for now. There would be time enough later to talk further. He and Alexia needed to get to his brother's reception.

## Seven

ALEXIA STOOD in the doorway and surveyed the scene before her. The barn was flooded with light. Tables were arranged throughout the open space, draped with white table-cloths. Flameless candles flickered from the center of each table. A band played instrumental music during dinner, which was a huge buffet spread that lined an entire wall. Catered by a local company, the food was home cooking at its finest. Chicken, steak, ribs, corn, potatoes, fresh bread. Alexia's mouth watered at the sight.

Near the head table, a smaller table held the wedding cake, which she'd made. A multi-layer extravaganza, covered in fondant and fresh flowers, Alexia was proud. It was the largest wedding cake she'd made yet. It touched her that Joy trusted her with such a monumental responsibility. Alexia worked hard to earn that trust. If the guests' comments were anything to go by, she'd more than achieved her goal.

*If only her parents could see her now.* They had been critical of her decision to accept her grandmother's inheritance and take over the bakery. If they could see her now, in this moment, with this cake, Alexia was sure they'd understand why this was so important to her. Baking was in her blood. Her destiny. The bakery, and the joy she brought to others through her work there, was so important.

She was dreading telling them about her and Cameron. They still operated under the hope that she'd "come to her senses" and return home to her comfortable, if not boring, job. Find a stable, meaning boring, man. She knew she never would. She wished they would realize that. It would make their relationship so much easier.

"You want a drink?" Cameron asked.

"Yes, please." Cameron passed her a flute of champagne. Alexia sipped the bubbly liquid slowly, savoring the texture of the carbonation on her tongue.

They stood at one end of the barn, the rustic charm of the scene before them. Alexia glanced around at the guests, all of whom were busy chatting and laughing while sipping their chosen drinks. It occurred to her that she and Cameron were on a first date of sorts. A reunion date. At a wedding.

Alexia could too easily imagine her and Cameron standing in front of an officiant, repeating vows to each other. Sipping champagne at their reception. Their wedding looked different in her imagination. They would marry at "their spot" on the property. Up on the hill overlooking Wildwood Falls. They'd say their vows looking over the town they loved and then celebrate with family and friends under large white tents. When it got dark, she and Cameron would climb in the back of his truck, in their wedding attire, drink champagne and watch the stars. A perfect wedding.

Joy bounded up to Alexia and gave her a hug. "Thank you for all your hard work. Everything is perfect. And that cake! Everyone is raving about how beautiful it is!"

Joy was glowing, and it wasn't from champagne. She'd confided to her bridesmaids earlier that she was expecting and was due in December. She'd needed to enlist their help in case a bout of morning sickness occurred. Thankfully, it hadn't, and Joy was free to soak up every minute of her special day.

"You're welcome! I appreciate you giving me the opportunity to make it. I'd love to do more special events."

"Oh, you will. Everyone has asked me about it. I'm sure you'll be flooded with calls on Monday."

Alexia heart soared at the possibility. Catering special events gave her the chance to use her creativity and try new things. "Thanks, Joy. Now go enjoy your party. And your groom," she said with a wink.

Joy laughed. "I will." She leaned down to whisper in Alexia's ear. "I'm glad you and Cameron finally realized you're meant for each other."

*Meant for each other.* Those words landed heavily in Alexia's chest. Not sure how to respond, she simply nodded. She and Cameron had just reunited. They didn't need the pressure of everyone else's expectations. She'd lived her whole life with the weight of disappointing her parents. The last thing she needed was to feel that way with her friends.

Oblivious to Alexia's worries, Joy gave her friend a hug before moving on to the next guests.

"Ready to sit down?" Cameron asked, having appeared at her elbow. His question pulled her back to the present moment.

"Yes, let's find our seats." They found their place cards, which led them to a table in the center of the room. Sarah and Griffin, as well as the rest of the bridal party that weren't family, sat with them.

The table soon filled, and conversation flowed. The band, which had been playing soft music during the cocktail hour, shifted to more upbeat selections. Soon everyone would be dancing.

Alexia glanced towards the head table in the front of the room. She glimpsed Luke's brother, William and Joy's cousin,

Hope, with heads bent low next to each other. Seemed like they were hitting it off. Alexia watched as Hope shook her head at William, then headed out the side door into the night. A moment later, William followed. That was a curious development.

Soon after, their table was called to the buffet line and Alexia and Cameron loaded their plates with delicious food. As soon as dinner ended, guests started dancing. Alexia looked longingly at the dance floor. She'd never danced with Cameron. She wasn't even sure he liked to dance. She realized how little she knew about the man she'd been in love with once.

Cameron followed her gaze, then reached over to touch her hand. "Do you want to dance?"

"Yes," she agreed readily. Cameron led her to the dance floor, and they swayed to a popular, upbeat song. On the next song, the music turned into a romantic ballad. Cameron pulled Alexia into his arms and easily led her around the dance floor.

She wound her arms around his neck and allowed her fingers to play with the hair at the nape of his neck. He circled her waist firmly, pulling her flush to his chest. She could smell his aftershave and the underlying scent of maleness that was so very Cameron.

Alexia could tell they were getting attention. To some it might seem sudden that they went from not speaking at all, to a public romantic dance. Except she knew this dance was years in the making. And in this moment, she couldn't bring herself to care what anyone else thought.

# Eight

A FEW DAYS LATER, Cameron pulled up to the curb of the Wildwood Falls International Airport. Alexia was going to visit her parents for the week. He'd hinted a few more times about joining her, but she rebuffed him each time. He didn't want to rush things, but it seemed he had been waiting for her all his life.

In his heart, he knew Alexia had to do this for herself. To deal with her parents and finally put her foot down about what she wanted. As much as Cameron wanted to go with her and support her, he understood why she had to do it alone.

In the weeks since their trip to Spokane, Alexia had experimented with several cake designs. She'd received several orders since Joy and Luke's wedding and spent hours excitedly planning the designs. Cameron volunteered happily to be a taste tester.

"You ready?" he asked, as he set her luggage on the sidewalk.

Alexia nodded, though her expression wasn't convincing. She looked terrified. "I'm as ready as I'll ever be."

"You'll do great. I'll be here when you get back."

He had big plans for this week. Watching Alexia go after her dreams had inspired him to take firm steps towards his own business. He had a heart to heart with his brother, William, about stepping back from ranch duties to pursue his woodworking. He'd secured a space at the Saturday Farmer's Market, which had an entire block dedicated to an artisan marketplace.

It was scary to branch out on his own, outside the security of his family's ranch, but he knew he was doing the right thing. He'd always have a place at Hudson Ranch. Now he had room to grow in new directions, as well.

He gave Alexia a hug and kiss and watched her enter the small, one-story airport, the first step on her journey to Seattle. He couldn't help but think back to that summer when she left, just like this. Cameron dropping her off at the curb, sure in his knowledge he'd see her again. Except he hadn't.

Cameron shook off the fear that history would repeat itself. They were grown adults now. They'd spent a few weeks to re-establish their connection, and the relationship was going smoothly. There was no reason to expect that Alexia would do anything besides come home next week as planned.

* * *

Visiting her parents had been more enjoyable than Alexia had expected. There was something comforting about being in her hometown, sleeping in her childhood bedroom, and visiting old friends. Alexia thought she might actually get through the entire trip without a lecture, except for the last day, when her parents unleashed all their unspoken concerns over brunch.

"Alexia, dear," her mom began, which was the first clue that her parents were mounting their campaign. "I really wish you'd consider moving home. You look so happy here. And you have your friends..."

"I have friends in Wildwood Falls."

"Yes, but I don't see how you can be happy there. Don't you miss city living?" Her mom gestured broadly to the view of Seattle behind them.

"I have the best of both worlds, mom. I get to live in a beautiful small town and come home to visit whenever I want."

"How will you support yourself working at a bakery? You spent four years getting the best education we could provide, so you could bake cakes all day?" Her mom was really laying it on thick.

"Mom. First of all, my degree helps me every day because I *own* my business. I make cakes, yes, and I love it. My cakes make people happy. My *career* makes people happy. I need you and dad to respect that. I'm not changing my mind. My home is in Wildwood Falls." *And my heart belongs to Cameron Hudson.*

Alexia didn't say that last part out loud. Establishing one boundary at a time was enough for her to manage.

Her mom dropped the subject, which Alexia took as a good sign. Later today, she'd have to bring up her relationship with Cameron. She couldn't leave Seattle without updating her parents on the development in her love life.

Rather than ask for the check at the end of the meal, her mom requested refills on their coffee. That was strange. Alexia was about to ask the reason for lingering, especially since her mom never lingered, when a familiar voice interrupted her thoughts.

"Alexia! What a surprise meeting you here!" Alexia looked up, stunned to see her ex-boyfriend, Chad, on the other side of the iron railing that separated their outdoor table from the street.

Her mom, the sneak. This was obviously a pre-arranged meeting. Except, was it? Because Chad had a gorgeous redhead on his arm. Both of them were dressed head to toe in designer fashion, as if they were on their way to somewhere much fancier than the restaurant Alexia and her parents favored.

A glance at her mom told Alexia that her mom was as shocked as she was to see the redhead. Chad smiled that megawatt smile that used to charm Alexia. It held no sway over her now.

"We're just heading for a reservation up the street. I was surprised when your mom reached out to say you were in town. Since we were already planning to be in the neighborhood, I decided to stop by and say hello."

"I didn't know you were seeing someone," her mom said, an accusatory tone tinging her voice.

"Mom," Alexia hissed. "I can't believe you planned this." Not only had her mom arranged for her to see her ex-boyfriend without telling her, she had apparently also arranged Alexia's most embarrassing moment to date.

Alexia had not gotten over the humiliation of Chad dumping her senior year of college because he needed someone "better suited to corporate dinners." Now, she was confronted with him and his attractive girlfriend.

"Honey, I didn't know," her mom replied in a stage whisper.

Alexia's ex looked back and forth between them. His date smirked, clearly enjoying the drama unfolding.

"Mom, that's it. I've officially had enough of your meddling. I'm dating someone. Seriously. You remember Cameron from when I used to visit grandma? He and I have been dating. We're in love."

Alexia stood up, throwing her napkin on the table in a show of rage. She turned to her ex and his smug date.

"I'm sorry my mom got you involved in this. I wish you all the best."

Then Alexia exited the patio. She walked as quickly as she could without looking back. She made it several blocks, fueled by anger, before realizing her parents were her ride back. Instead of returning to the restaurant, she ordered a car on her ride share app. She texted her dad, so her parents didn't worry.

Once she made it to her childhood room, the tentative control she'd held over her emotions broke and she collapsed on her bed. Hot tears spilled down her cheeks. Why did her mom have to always meddle? And assume she knew what was best for Alexia?

And why did Alexia have to announce she and Cameron were in love? They hadn't been together long enough for those words. Except Alexia knew she was in love with Cameron. She had been since the summer she was fourteen and she was even more so now.

When a knock sounded on her bedroom door awhile later, Alexia wasn't surprised. What she didn't expect to find was her father instead of her mother who opened the door.

"Dad? Did mom send you to do her dirty work?"

Her dad laughed, a low rumble in his barrel chest. "No, honey, she figured you needed some space before she talked with you. I came to see if you're ok."

He sat down on the side of her bed, as he used to do when she had nightmares as a child. He placed his hand gently on her head in his familiar way to offer comfort.

Alexia was transported back in time. No matter how much time passed, one always became a child again with one's parents.

"I'm ok, Dad. I just wish mom would accept that I'm not moving home. I have my own life. I'm happy."

"Your mom wants the best for you and sometimes that

comes across as pushy. We both want you to be happy. If you say you're happy, then that's good enough for us."

"Thanks, Dad."

"So, this Cameron. Is he good enough for our little girl?"

Alexia laughed. "Oh dad, he is. He's wonderful. And I love him."

Her dad hugged Alexia tight. "I can't wait to meet him."

# Nine

CAMERON CHECKED his phone for the tenth time in an hour. Alexia had texted to say she was extending her trip by a few days to work things out with her parents. He couldn't help but worry that a few days would turn into forever.

His brother, Luke, shook his head. "You've got it bad, dude."

Cameron looked up from his phone. "I don't. I'm just looking for an update. Alexia was booking a new flight today."

"Uh, huh. Help me load this arch into the truck. Lovesick or not, you have a farmer's market to attend."

Luke had offered to help load the truck with Cameron for the Farmer's Market. Luke had a table representing the Hudson Ranch beef, so was headed into town, anyway.

Cameron was looking forward to his first official activity in his new business. Word of mouth from Luke and Joy's wedding had already put his work in high demand and he would have no trouble making a profit in his first month of operations.

He took issue with his brother's assessment of his current emotional state, though. Cameron was not lovesick. He loved

Alexia, but knew she'd come back. This was nothing like when they were teenagers. Was it? He wished he could brush off his fears as easily as his brother could.

"You think she'll come back, right?" he asked his brother. "Her parents won't convince her to stay?"

Luke shot Cameron a sharp glance. "Alexia owns a business here. She loves you, for some unknown reason. She'll be back."

Cameron shoved his brother's shoulder in payback for the slight.

"You really think she loves me?"

"Seriously? Anyone that looks at the two of you together knows you 're ridiculously in love."

Cameron hesitated. "We haven't said the words yet."

Luke scoffed. "Actions speak louder than words, brother. And both your actions clearly say you're in love."

Cameron grinned. "You think? Because I have this idea..."

* * *

Alexia wasn't surprised when Cameron met her at the airport. She was surprised when he held flowers. Her heart skipped a beat at the sight of him waiting for her at baggage claim, flowers in hand.

"What's this?" she asked.

"Just a token of my appreciation. I missed you. I can't tell you how happy I am to see you home again."

Home. Yes, Wildwood Falls was her home. As enjoyable as her time in Seattle was, she'd always think of Wildwood Falls as home. In part because Cameron was here. And Cameron was quickly becoming her favorite idea of home.

He helped her load her luggage into the extended cab of his truck, then gave her a hand up into the passenger seat.

He pulled out of the airport and, rather than taking the

road that would lead to Alexia's house, he took the road leading to the Hudson Ranch.

"Where are we going?"

Cameron smiled. "You'll see. I promise you'll like it."

After a few minutes, he steered the car into Burger on the Range, joining the drive thru queue.

"Seriously, Cameron, what's up? We're stopping for dinner?"

"Yes, that's the start."

"The start?"

"You'll see," he replied with a wink.

At the drive-up window, Cameron placed their usual order, then drove towards the ranch. Their familiar routine. He was obviously bringing her to watch the sunset. Romantic.

Alexia's heart leapt in her chest. Cameron cared, even though she'd had to delay her return. He waited for her. She twirled a strand of her hair as she watched Cameron in the driver's seat. His expression gave nothing away about his feelings, but Alexia knew he must care. Her worries about his reaction to her delayed trip evaporated and she sat back to enjoy the ride.

She'd had time to think while in Seattle and was even more sure of her feelings for him now that she'd returned. When they got to their spot, she would tell him her feelings. He deserved to hear her say the words.

When they reached the crest of the hill, rather than the empty field she expected, Alexia was greeted with an unexpected scene.

A large blanket had been spread out over the grass. A wicker picnic basket was set on it, as well as a bucket filled with ice and champagne. Pillows were strewn artfully on the blanket.

The most impressive feature was a large, carved arch that framed the view of the valley below. At first glance, she thought it was the one from Joy and Luke's wedding, but when she got out of the truck for a closer look, she saw that it was different. It contained elaborate floral carvings as the other one had. Instead of Joy and Luke's initials and wedding date, the top of the arch contained Alexia and Cameron's names, with a blank space below. A date yet to be filled in?

The breath left Alexia's lungs when she realized he'd carved this for her. In the week she'd been at her parents, he'd carved an entire arch dedicated to their love.

"Oh, Cameron. This is beautiful," she exclaimed as she ran her hands lovingly over the wood.

"It was a labor of love," he replied.

"Cameron," she whispered as tears spilled over. "Cameron, I love you so much."

Cameron pulled her into a long hug. "I love you, too." He stepped back, setting her away from him for a moment. Alexia felt the loss of him and moved to close the gap. He shook his head, indicating she should stay where she was.

"Alexia," Cameron began. "I've loved you since we were fourteen."

"I've loved you, too," she replied. She stepped towards him again, but before she reached him, he did the most shocking thing.

He went down on his knees, pulling a small velvet box out of his pocket as he did. "I have loved you since we were teenagers and I will love you always. Will you do me the honor of marring me?"

Alexia's tears were falling in earnest now. "Yes, yes, oh yes, Cameron, I'll marry you."

He slipped the ring on her finger with shaking hands. Once he'd secured the classic diamond solitaire on her finger, he stood up and engulfed her in an enormous hug.

"Forever," he whispered against her hair. "We have forever together."

# Epilogue

ALEXIA'S BAKERY smelled like fall. Nutmeg, cinnamon, and pumpkin spice wafted through the space. Today was the annual Wildwood Falls Autumn festival. She had outdone herself, baking for the occasion.

Soon the shop would be filled with customers as they walked Main St and sampled all the fall cheer the businesses in town offered.

This was the first year Alexia truly felt a part of the celebration. With Cameron at her side, Wildwood Falls finally felt like home.

"It smells amazing in here," the man in question said as he entered.

"Woof!" a furry companion, Toffee, added. The golden retriever puppy had joined their family a few weeks ago once they'd settled in together in her grandmother's cozy craftsman style home a short walk from Main St.

Alexia had hired a few part time workers, in addition to reliable Mabel, since her return from Seattle. She had big plans to expand her custom cake business and needed the help with the day to day of running the bakery. Two of her new employees were here now, gearing up for a busy day.

Which meant that Alexia was free to enjoy the Fall Festival with Cameron and Toffee. Instead of working behind the bakery counter, she could walk the streets of town with her fiancé and enjoy the fall ambience in Wildwood Falls. A stop at Joy's Christmas shop was mandatory, to check in on her friend and rub her growing belly. She was due in December, just in time for Christmas. Cameron and Alexia couldn't wait to be aunts. And maybe add to the family themselves, in the near future.

Cameron had moved off the ranch and in with Alexia, so they had plenty of space for a family to grow. He had rented a small studio space a few blocks away to sell his wood crafts. He still used the old barn on Hudson Ranch to craft his creations, but now he had a location in town to cater to the tourists who snapped up his smaller works. The business had even gotten custom orders from out of state. His small side business was shaping up to be a full-time career.

Alexia couldn't be happier with how everything had turned out. They'd decided to marry quickly and their own wedding day was fast approaching. An October wedding outdoors, under that beautiful wooden arch, would be the perfect way to start their forever. They planned their honeymoon for Victoria, Canada and had agreed to stop to see her parents on the way. Alexia's parents had come around to the idea of her making a home in Wildwood Falls and had visited once since the engagement. They were excited to come to the wedding as well. Once they'd realized that Wildwood Falls and Cameron made her happy, the were one hundred percent behind her decision.

Cameron's arms came around Alexia as she stood pondering their good fortune. "I love you, Alexia."

She leaned her head back against his chest. "I love you, too, Cameron."

"Forever," he replied.

"Yes, forever," she agreed.

* * *

More Wildwood Falls awaits in Christmas Crush on the Rancher. Meet Cameron's brother, Will, as he falls hard for Hope!

Thank you for reading! Learn more about my stories in Heather Scarlett's VIP reader group!

Heather Scarlett lives in Southern California, although her heart is in Montana where she lived for six wonderful years. She loves big sky, wide open spaces, and cowboys. Heather writes smart and sexy small-town romance that is equal parts sweet and emotionally satisfying. Her heroines are strong and sassy and her heroes are rugged and capable. Heather's stories are family focused and relationship driven.